MW01449492

This is the back of the book. You wouldn't want to spoil a great ending!

This book is printed "manga-style," in the authentic Japanese right-to-left format. Since none of the artwork has been flipped or altered, readers get to experience the story just as the creator intended. You've been asking for it, so TOKYOPOP® delivered: authentic, hot-off-the-press, and far more fun!

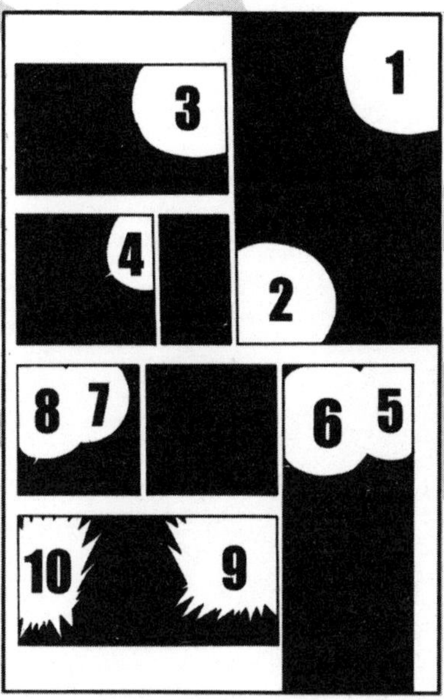

DIRECTIONS

If this is your first time reading manga-style, here's a quick guide to help you understand how it works.

It's easy... just start in the top right panel and follow the numbers. Have fun, and look for more 100% authentic manga from TOKYOPOP®!

THE MANGA REVOLUTION · LEADING · THE MANGA REVOLUTION · LEADING

漫画革命

Dead Animals Need Love Too

Skelanimals
It's a Wonderful Afterlife

When the wintry winds start to blow
Kit gets sick of the cold and the snow
This poor cat is chilled to the bone.
Now she's cold, quite dead, and alone.
Until each of her pals do their part,
To help warm a dead kitty's heart!

Available now from fine retailers and book chains everywhere!

® & © Skelanimals, LLC.

THE WORLD IS SO MUCH MORE FUN TO THE OUTSIDE OBSERVER!

THE SECRET NOTES OF
LADY KANOKO™
heh heh heh
Lady Kanoko's Notes for 'Good' Boys and Girls
Volume 1
Ririko Tsujita
TOKYO POP

Kanoko doesn't mind being alone in the class room because her one and only goal is to be a completely objective bystander who observes as events unfold around her. Steamy love triangles, secret affairs between students and teachers, the backbiting politics of teenage girls...everything is jotted down in her **secret notebook**!

© 2008 Ririko Tsujita / HAKUSENSHA, INC.

FOR MORE INFORMATION VISIT: www.TOKYOPOP.com

FROM THE CREATOR OF chibi Vampire
AiON
Volume 1
Yuna Kagesaki
TOKYOPOP

EVIL MERMAIDS and MIND-CONTROLLING PARASITES lurk in a seaside town!

After losing both parents in a car accident, **Tatsuya Tsugawa** tries to fulfill his father's dying wish of becoming an upstanding man. At school, he attempts to save a girl named **Seine** from bullies, but she refuses flat-out and even says that she likes being bullied! What will Tatsuya do when his good will and earnest efforts lead him into a twisted, wicked fantasy world?

FROM THE CREATOR OF chibi Vampire

T TEEN AGE 13+

© 2009 YUNA KAGESAKI / FUJIMISHOBO.

FOR MORE INFORMATION VISIT: www.TOKYOPOP.com

PUTTING THE VAN IN VANQUISH
WATCH IT FOR FREE ON HULU.COM!
STARRING NARUTO VOICE ACTOR YURI LOWENTHAL
VAN VON HUNTER
TOKYOPOP
OFFICIAL SELECTION FANTASIA 2010
hulu
TOKYO POP

12,000 MILES...20 CITIES...8 WEEKS...
6 STUDENTS...5 FAN CONS...ONE SEARCH...
AND A WHOOOOLE LOT OF POCKY...
TOKYOPOP PRESENTS
AMERICA'S GREATEST OTAKU
WATCH IT WEEKLY AT
WWW.HULU.COM
PRODUCED BY TOKYOPOP
WWW.GREATESTOTAKU.COM
hulu

ぶべっ

I'M A GUY...
IS THAT GOING TO BE A PROBLEM?
Extra-manly voice.

IN THE NEXT VOLUME OF VB Rose
AFTER A LONG TIME APART, MITSUYA AND TSUYU ARE FINALLY REUNITED...
MEANWHILE, THINGS BEGIN TO CHANGE FOR AGEHA AND YUKARI AS WELL...?!
VB ROSE VOL. 13 COMING SOON!
JOIN US NEXT TIME!
SEE YOU LATER!

Bonus Page
AGEHA THE PIRATE
The dress and the hat that Ageha is wearing are from Kaie-san's brand "Triple Fortune." Plus, this is a collaboration piece by "Triple Fortune" and a magazine. Anna Tsuchiya was wearing it!
Wow, Kaie-san I want to dra this outfit!
How about you make Ageha wear it?
I can?!
She showed me the actual dress in pictures before.
So there you have it! I made Ageha we it! Kaie-san, thank you so much! On top of that, she gave me the whole outfit as a gif I'm so happy! So I have it at home.
I'm going to set it up on a mannequin as decoration. I hope you enjoy the frills and sparkles on this page!
日高万里。2008
Banri Hidaka, 2008

A HUMONGOUS PIECE OF LETTUCE CUT LENGTH-WISE.
Cheese
Ham
The Treble Clef crackers were the only thing "Maestro" about it.
HA HA HA HA HA HA!! THIS IS THE SAME FOOD I'D GIVE TO SAPPHIRE!!
Ha ha ha ha, this is awesome! This rocks!
IF I WANTED TO CHOP UP FOOD, I COULD HAVE DONE IT IN MY OWN KITCHEN!
This is the same as eating at home!!
IT WAS THE MOST OUT-RAGEOUS(?) SALAD I'VE EVER SEEN.
Babi-san's fluffy white bunny.
Maniacal laughter.
Pfft!
Kaie-san cut it for us.
Grrrr!
She's pretty good with a knife.
AFTER THAT, MY FRIENDS HAD A SURPRISE FOR ME, AND WE HAD A GREAT TIME. ♡
I only got to show you guys the tip of the iceberg...just that many things happened in three days!
TREASURE ALL THE EXPERIENCES LIFE GIVES YOU.
Since I'm always at home facing my desk...
...the few times I go out are so fun!
I'LL SEE YOU ALL NEXT TIME IN V.B. ROSE VOLUME 13. ♡

Banri Hidaka's Everyday Heaven / End

AND OF COURSE ...
Aghh...
I spilled my drink.
I poured my drink down my face.
Oops?
Whoa!
NOW WE UNDERSTAND WHY YOU CARRY AROUND FOUR HANDKERCHIEFS.
Lacks the skills to do anything but draw manga.
Did your clothes get wet?
Yes.
Heh heh, I think the problem is I'm ADD.
Lame.
IT TURNED OUT THAT THE MOST SHOCKING DISH OF ALL WAS "MAESTRO'S CAESAR SALAD."
This is so much fun!
I'm glad you're enjoying yourself.
HERE'S A KNIFE FOR YOUR SALAD.
The pasta was indeed very good.

WHILE WE WERE CHIT-CHATTING AT KAIE-SAN'S HOUSE...
So I'm thinking of using this design here. Mwa ha ha.
わく わく
Wow, that looks exciting!
...A BUSINESS PARTNER OF HERS NAMED "BABI" DROPPED BY.
"Tokyo Bro" Number 2
SHE'S ALSO VERY GOOD-LOOKING, TALL AND TOTALLY FUNNY ON THE INSIDE!!
キラ キラ キラ
It's good to see you again.
HIDAKA! ♪
I'M GLAD! YOU DON'T LOOK LIKE YOU LOST TOO MUCH WEIGHT.
BABI-SAN?!
Last time I saw her, she was a redhead! Now she's a blond.
HEY, BRO...! I DIDN'T HEAR ABOUT THIS!
きっぱり
BK IS ALWAYS TOGETHER.
What are you talking about.
もきゃー
Stupid Hidaka!
※ (B) for Babi-san and (K) for Kaie-san = BK
AFTER THAT, WE MET UP WITH YURIKO-SAN, WHO IS A LIBRARIAN.
I see you finished your work. Awesome!
Thanks, Sis! I missed you so much!
Arf!
I call Yuriko-san "My Tokyo Sister"
Marry me.
WE ALL HAVE COMPLETELY DIFFERENT JOBS AND PERSONALITIES, BUT SOMEHOW WE GET ALONG. SO THE FOUR OF US WENT OUT TO DINNER. ♪
WE HEADED OUT TO IKEBUKURO, IN SEARCH OF A PARTICULAR THEMED RESTAURANT THAT WOULD ONLY BE IN BUSINESS FOR A LIMITED TIME. IT WAS CALLED...
..."THE MAGICIAN OF THE OPERA HOUSE."
Theme restaurant virgin.
Wow, whatta huge menu!
ドキ ドキ
It goes with the theme.
Hee hee.
We heard that their pasta is really good.
Yep, yep.
Let's go inside.
Menu
THE MENU GOES SOME-THING LIKE THIS...
Christine's Something-or-other...
The Phantom's Blah Blah...
The Knight of the Rose...
Cinderella's Whatchamacallit...
Maestro's Caesar Salad...
Can't I get the "normal" salad?
No, half the fun is telling the waitress the funny name!
Yeah...
Wow!
ANYWAY, THE WHOLE MENU WAS LIKE THAT.

Banri Hidaka's Everyday Heaven

AFTER THE MAY DEADLINE FOR MY NEW SERIES, "BERRY BERRY," I WENT TO TOKYO FOR TWO DAYS AND THREE NIGHTS FOR A MEETING.
I'm finally done!
Kaie-san, are you free on X day?!
Yeah, I'm free.
Are you free up until the next afternoon, too?!
Sure!
Yay!
THE MEETING TOOK PLACE ON THE SECOND NIGHT...
...SO I HUNG OUT WITH A FRIEND ON THE FIRST DAY.
THAT FRIEND OF MINE IS "KAIE-SAN," A FASHION DESIGNER.
She's a really awesome designer who creates weddin dresses and stage costumes and hats. She also has her own Gothic Lolita brand.
Hey, come in.
She's got a lot of sides, and I like that in a person.
NOT ONLY IS SHE BEAUTIFUL ON THE OUTSIDE, SHE'S A REALLY FUNNY PERSON ON THE INSIDE!
You want some pulpy orange juice?
WE WORK TOGETHER FREQUENTLY, BUT WE'RE ALSO GOOD FRIENDS.
Sign me up.
I CALL HER MY "TOKYO BRO."
OVER THE PAST YEAR, HER HAIR HAS GONE FROM BLACK → BLONDE → SILVER.

I'LL NEVER LET GO OF THIS HAND...
...EVER AGAIN.
V.B. Rose 12 End

THANKS FOR COMING WITH ME.
Ha ha...
THANK YOU FOR TAKING ME OUT OF THERE.

YUKARI-KUN...
...YOU REALLY ARE A GUY AFTER ALL.
You're not huggable.
さわ さわ
GROPE
LET'S GET OUTTA HERE, AGEHA.
SEE YOU TWO LATER! ♡
Screw you, Mitsu!
Hmph!
むくっ
Oh...
MITSUYA-KUN, ARE YOU ALL RIGH--
TSUYU.
BADUM
YES?!

Whisper
YOU DUMMY.
"THANK YOU, YUKARI-KUN."
RIGHT BACK AT YOU, MAN.

IT'S HARD TO TAKE YOUR VIOLENT THREATS SERIOUSLY WHEN YOU'RE DRESSED SO ELEGANTLY.
Tee hee.
YOU BAST--

I SHOULD SHOW MY GRATITUDE, TOO.
This
I'M SO GRATEFUL THAT I WANT TO HANG AN SUPER-ENLARGED PICTURE OF KIMONO YUKARI-KUN IN THE STORE.
Beautifu
OH MY GOSH!
THAT'S NOT GRATITUDE, THAT'S TORTURE!!
I ought to wring your neck!

JUST...
...THANK YOU SO MUCH.
THANK YOU FOR GIVING ME COURAGE.
THANK YOU!

むぎゅー
OH!
SORRY!
You're suffocating me...
My hug was too snug.
TSUYU?
AGEHA-CHAN.
ARISAKA-KUN.
MITSUYA-KUN.
THERE'S ...
...SO MANY THINGS THAT I WANT TO SAY...
...BUT I JUST...
...CAN'T GET THE WORDS... OUT...

YOINK
Hey!
KAZUHA-SAN.
THAT'S MY JOB.
TOTALLY TRUE.
LOOKS LIKE YOU ONLY HAVE ROOM IN YOUR HEART FOR TSUYU-CHAN.
Whatever.
ALL RIGHT, I'M GOING TO HEAD BACK!
LET ME KNOW WHEN SOMETHING EXCITING HAPPENS AGAIN.
Sugimoto is waiting for me.
Bye bye!
GOTTA SAY, THAT IS ONE TAKE-CHARGE LADY.
ISN'T SHE? ☆
UH ...
UM...

YOU DIDN'T CAUSE ANY TROUBLE FOR ANYONE.
NN ...
TH...
THANK YOU... SO MUCH.

SHE AGREED TO HELP OUT AS SOON AS WE ASKED. ♪
YEP.
MATERNITY LEAVE IS BORING.
BLUNT
WATCHING YOU GUYS IN ACTION WAS PRETTY FUN, THOUGH.
She was watching Mitsu and Tsuyu's getaway from the cafe.
Ah, young love.
AND TSUYU-CHAN...
YES?
Eep.
...YOUR FATHER AND YOUR AUNT...
...CAME OUT LOOKING RELIEVED AND HAPPY.
DON'T WORRY.

K... KAZUHA-SAN?!!
YO!
WH...WHAT BRINGS YOU HERE?!
HMM?
And Hina-chan, too!!
I DRESSED THEM AND DID THEIR MAKE-UP.
にしし
Thank you...
Those two hooligans.

HE SUCCESSFULLY BEWITCHED YOUR EX-ALMOST-FIANCE WITH HIS EXQUISITE BEAUTY! ☆
Poor guy's completely incapacitated. ♡
きゃるん♡
AGEHA!!
Aghhhhhh!
TR...
IT...
BU...
Translation: "But it's true!"
ギリギリギリ
SCRATCH
SCRATCH
Iron claw style.
I WISH I COULD HAVE SEEN IT.
BADUM BADUM
TREMBLE
TREMBLE
SOMEONE DID A NICE JOB ON YOUR MAKE-UP, YUKARI.
Ha ha ha.
I KNOW, RIGHT? ♡
I'm amazed. ♪
...

WE HAD SEKUGUCHI ASK THE OWNER TO LET US IN AS WAITERS...
Aww, Yukarin is asking daddy for a favor!
HUG
Hey! You're not my dad!!
...SO THAT WE COULD LET YOU ESCAPE SMOOTHLY.
So this is the situation...
BOW
Thank you for your understanding.
I can't let an ill-arranged marriage take place in my establishment!!
Leave it to me!!
The owner was very cooperative.
YOU GUYS...
SO, WHY THE KIMONO?
Erk!
BADUM
BADUM
...

YOU DIDN'T TELL HER?
IT WAS ON A NEED-TO-KNOW BASIS.
SHE NEEDS TO KNOW.
TSUYU ...
CHECK OUT THIS PICTURE OF YUKARI-KUN CHANGING INTO THE KIMONO.
Ageha texted it to him.
Here, take a look.
I HAVE A PICTURE OF HIM IN A WAITER COSTUME, TOO.
Hee hee hee.
P... PLEASE SEND ME ALL THE PICTURES!!
WHAT THE HELL, YOU GUYS?!
I'LL CUT TO THE CHASE.
Hmph.
SEKIGUCHI IS PALS WITH THE OWNER OF THAT PLACE.

カシャッ
SNAP
Save.
Save.
Next one.
Next one.
BIP
Come on!
Come on!
BIP
BIP
WHAT ARE YOU TAKING PICTURES FOR?!
Hand it over.
No.
I DON'T UNDERSTAND YOU.
I-I CAN'T HELP MYSELF, YOU'RE JUST TOO BEAUTIFUL RIGHT NOW...
CLENCH
I'M THE ONE WHO DOESN'T UNDERSTAND WHAT'S GOING ON!
?!
S...
...SO...
...WHAT HAPPENED AFTER I LEFT?!

WHO IS THIS...
... ORGEOUS ERSON?!
GOOD THING YOUR ARRANGED MARRIAGE MEETING WENT SOUTH.
Artisan!
Oh!
Artisan!
A...
HUH?
What is it?
... ARISAKA-KUN?!!

SOUNDS LIKE EVERYTHING WENT WELL, THEN!
YOU CAN SAY THAT AGAIN!!
BUT SERIOUSLY, HOW DID YOU GET ALL THAT INFORMATION?
DON'T UNDERESTIMATE ME.
Not gonna ask what he did for it...
W...WHAT HAPPENED BACK THERE?!
HEY! ARTISAN!

OH!
RING-LEADER
YUKARI-KUN AND AGEHA-CHAN ARE ALMOST AT THE PARK.
REALLY?!
BAM
BAM
BAM
AGEHA-CHAN!!
Yaaaay!
イエー
HEYA! ♡ EVERYTHING'S BEEN TAKEN CARE OF, TSUYU-SAN! ♪

MY LIFE IS BETTER OFF BECAUSE SHE'S IN IT.
BY THE WAY...
...WHO COMPILED THIS RESEARCH?
?
DEEDLE DEE

NO.
DADDY, I LOVE YOU!
DADDY!
WHAT YOU DID WAS SET ME UP...
...WITH THE BEST DAUGHTER IN THE WORLD.

AFTER ALL...
...I SET YOU UP WITH A TERRIBLE WIFE.
HMM.
I wonder why things always go wrong when I'm trying to set my family up?

MATCHMAKING DOES HAPPEN TO BE MY FAVORITE *HOBBY*, THOUGH.
BLUNT
You see where I'm coming from ...
TSUYU-CHAN HAS ALWAYS BEEN SUCH A HOMEBODY.
DECISIONS HAVE BEEN SUCH A STRUGGLE FOR HER, TOO.
I WANTED TO HELP HER OUT.
OR AM I NOT ALLOWED TO CARE WHAT HAPPENS TO HER?
I JUST WANT HER...
...TO BE HAPPY.

BUT WHY DIDN'T YOU LET THE CAT OUT OF THE BAG?
YOU SHOULD HAVE TOLD ME SHE HAD A BOYFRIEND!
AUNTIE LIKES TO KNOW THESE THINGS.
And he's a looker, too!
A-CHOO!
POUT
POUT
SIS...
I THOUGHT YOU WANTED TO CROSS TSUYU OFF YOUR LIST.
I LOVE MY NIECE WAY TOO MUCH TO TREAT HER LIKE THAT!
How could you say that?!
Am I some kind of match-making monster to you?
Eh?
Rrrgh!

ひゅ
WHOOSH
KASUMI-SAN, I'M SORRY!
I DIDN'T DO A THOROUGH ENOUGH BACKGROUND CHECK!
Oooh!
PLEASE... DON'T WORRY ABOUT IT.
STILL ...
...I'M GLAD THIS HAP-PENED.
Heh heh.
IF ONLY BECAUSE IT GOT YOU TO SPEAK YOUR MIND FOR ONCE.
THAT'S BE-CAUSE ...
...I LOVE MY DAUGHTER SO MUCH.

I THINK...
...WE'RE BETTER OFF WITHOUT YOU.
LET'S GO, SIS.
PITTER PATTER
OH!
COMING, COMING!
にょ
YOU DO REALIZE ...
...THE WEDDING'S PERMANENTLY CANCELED, RIGHT?

FIDGET
FIDGET
W... WELL...
OH MY!!
YOU MENTIONED THE MANAGEMENT OF OUR KIMONO SHOP EARLIER...!
YOU MUST HAVE BEEN PLANNING ON TAKING ADVANTAGE OF US!!
My goodness, how atrocious!
Bingo ☆
AH...

MS. ICHIHA --
YOUR STOCKS HAVE PLUMMETED AND YOU'VE ACCRUED A HEAP OF DEBT.
ド
YOUR SON IS SUSPECTED OF EMBEZZLING YOUR COMPANY'S MONEY...
...AND HAS NUMEROUS COUNTS OF SEXUAL HARRASSMENT ON HIS RECORD.
キッ
THIS IS DAMNING EVIDENCE.
BUT I WOULD LIKE TO HEAR...
...YOUR OWN WORDS ON THE MATTER.

I'VE BROUGHT...
...A DELIVERY FOR ICHIHASHI-SAMA...
...FROM THE FRONT DESK.
HERE IT IS.
CAN'T YOU SEE WE'RE IN THE MIDDLE OF A DISCUSSION RIGHT NOW?!
?

Episode 71

STILL ...
...I HATE THAT I RAN OUT ON DAD AND AUNTIE.
I HOPE THEY'RE OKAY.
NOOO PROB-LEM-O.
I'VE GOT IT ALL FIGURED OUT.
MS. ICHIHASHI, CAN YOU PLEASE EXPLAIN WHAT IS GOING ON?!
...
ARE YOU LISTEN-ING TO ME?!
AGEHA-CHAN WILL SMOOTHE THINGS OUT.
AHEM.
PARDON ME.
I MUST INTERRUPT.

Wooo...
WHAT?!
HE'S BEEN TO COURT FOR SEXUAL HARASS-MENT?!
YEP.
HE CAN'T KEEP HIS HANDS OFF THE LADIES.
THAT'S PART OF THE REASON WHY...
...THEY CAME ALL THE WAY OUT HERE FROM TOKYO.

HELLO, BEAUTIFUL.
ぎゅーっ
SQUEEZE
WOULD YOU DO ME THE HONOR OF ENLIGHTENING ME WITH YOUR DELIGHTFUL NAME?
Mumble
I'm ...
WHAT?
I'M A GUY...
IS THAT GOING TO BE A PROBLEM?
Extra-manly voice.

!
SUYU-SA--
?!
It's someone else?!
Found it.
WHAM
WHAT IS WITH TODAY?!!
...
Ouch!
WHAT'S THE BIG IDEA, SITTING IN THE MIDDLE OF--

...ARE YOU THE KIND OF GIRL WHO HIDES RAVISHING BEAUTY BEHIND A PAIR OF GLASSES?
You mustn't be so shy.
SIR...
...DON'T YOU HAVE A BRIDE TO CHASE AFTER?
OH! THAT'S RIGHT! WE'LL SPEAK AGAIN LATER.
MAKES SENSE THAT SOMEONE SO FULL OF HOT AIR WOULD BE AN AIRHEAD.
"Later"? Not on your life.
I'VE GOT ONE MORE JOB LEFT TO DO. ♪
OOPSIE.

Bwah!
SCHING
OH MY! ARE YOU ALL RIGHT, SIR?!
HAVE YOU HURT YOURSELF?!
I'M FINE!
IF YOU'LL EXCUSE ME, I'M IN A HURRY --
ARE YOU...
YOU DON'T SEEM THE TYPE, AND YET...
WH... WHAT?!
DID HE FIGURE OUT THAT I'VE BEEN SABOTAGING HIM?

...IS GOING DOWN THE PATH I WAL
WITH HIM.
TSUYU-SAN?!
THAT BOY...
...
...WASN'T HE MITSUYA KUROMINE-KUN...?
ババババ
THUD
THUD
THUD
だっ
WHAT IS GOING ON, MS. ICHIHASHI?!
MICHIHIKO-CHAN! GO GET HER!
UMM...
O... OKAY!
ぱたぱたぱたぱた
PATTER
PATTER

...BUT MY LIFE...

"I WANT YOU TO COME WITH ME..."
"...OF YOUR OWN FREE WILL."
I'M SORRY, DAD...

TSUYU!
LET'S GO!

WHO ARE YOU, YOUNG MAN?!
MITSUYA-KU--

"IT'S GOING TO BE OKAY."
TSU...
SO, DO YOU HAVE ANY DESIRE TO EXPAND...
...YOUR KIMONO SHOP?
MY SON IS INTERESTED IN MANAGEMENT AS WELL.
YOUR BUSINESS WOULD BE IN GOOD HANDS--
ざわ
...sir!
EXCUSE ME, SIR?!
バ A THUD
バ A THUD
バ A THUD
バ A THUD
バ A THUD
THAT ROOM IS RESERVED--!
PLEASE WAIT!
ガラッ

Psst
Enjoy your tea.
SLIDE

MICHIHIKO-SAN?
AREN'T YOU GETTING A LITTLE AHEAD OF YOURSELF THERE?
AH, I'M SORRY. IT'S A HABIT OF MINE.
THAT'S MY SON, ALWAYS AN OVER-ACHIEVER.
Ho ho ho.
Tsuyu-chan hasn't even said a word yet.
...
MITSUYA-KUN...
ぎゅう…っ
TAP
TAP
?!

This volume only has two columns! So if you're looking for more Banri Hidaki updates, don't miss the Everyday Heaven feature at the end of the book! Hey, don't just skip to the end--enjoy the story, too!

Thanks a ton, all you folks who have helped me create this manga, both on the front lines and behind the scenes.

After I finished drawing Episode 71 (the last episode of this volume), I started this new series called "Berry Berry." It's about twins. I love twins!

I'm Kurumi.
I'm Sarahime.

So, I'm about to start work on Episode 72 now :) I'm planning to complete the story of V.B. Rose in volume 14. I'll be putting my all into this last arc, so please come along for the ride!

I'd love to hear your thoughts on volume 12!

attn: Banri Hidaka
c/o TOKYOPOP
5900 Wilshire
Blvd, #2000
Los Angeles, CA 90036

I'll be waiting.

...IS A PEACEFUL ONE...
...WHERE WE'VE SETTLED DOWN TO A MARRIAGE FULL OF TRANQUILITY.
Whoa, buddy.
ISN'T THAT MOVING A LITTLE FAST THERE?
Spy number 2
RUSTLE
KUROMINE-SAN, NOW IT'S YOUR TURN!!
Go!
CLICK
BEEP

ニコ
AGEHA-CHAN?!!
Um...
Um...
Pardon me.
Thank you.
TSUYU-SAN.
THE LIFE I ENVISION WITH YOU IN IT...

...IS IT RUDE THAT I FEEL KIND OF GROSSED OUT...?
I HOPE YOU CAN FORGIVE ME. I'M SO NERVOUS THAT I'M TRIPPING OVER OWN MY TONGUE.
NO, YOU'RE NOT!
EXCUS ME.
YOUR TEA IS SERVE
はっ
MAYBE THAT'LL KEEP HIM QUIET FOR A BIT!!
HOLD ON.
THAT VOICE...
NO, IT DIDN'T STOP!!
He comes b it naturall though.
Aghhh!
NOT AFFECTED
BUT I THOUGHT ABOUT IT LONG AND HARD.
SLIDE

AFTER HE SAW YOUR DAUGHTER'S PICTURES, MY SON COULDN'T WAIT TO MEET HER.
Ho ho ho.
Verbal warfare?!
MOTHER!
I'M SORRY.
MY MOTHER GETS SO EXCITED THAT SHE TALKS AND TALKS.
OH NO, DON'T WORRY.
BUT...
...IT'S TRUE THAT I'VE BEEN LOOKING FORWARD TO MEET YOU.
YOU ARE EVEN MORE CHARMING IN PERSON THAN IN YOUR PICTURES.
WAIT ...
I DON'T KNOW HOW TO SAY THIS...BUT THIS IS THE FIRST TIME THAT I'VE FELT THIS WAY.

SO, MY BOY MICHIHIKO STUDIED ECONOMICS AT TOKYO UNIVERSITY...
Ho ho ho.
...AND AFTER GRADUATING, HE ENTERED A MOST PRESTIGIOUS BROKERAGE FIRM.
BLAH BLAH BLAH BLAH BLAH BLAH
He's such a sweet and caring boy...
...He even volunteered to do accounting for my husband and I when he became concerned for our health.
I just can't say enough what a wonderful and caring son he is!
SHE SPEWS WORDS LIKE HER MOUTH'S A MACHINE GUN...
BLAH BLAH BLAH AH BLAH BLAH BLAH
MOTHER
YOU DO PLAN TO LET ME HAVE A WORD IN EDGEWISE, DON'T YOU?
OH MY! I'M SORRY, DARLING. OF COURSE.
TSUYU-SAN.
Y... YES?

カコン
TONK
カコーン。
TONK

He takes customer service very seriously!
HA HA HA! YOU'RE WORKING SO HARD!
DAMN YOU, MITSU.
I'LL HAVE A COFFEE.
... DON'T GET OFFENDED, 'KAY?
BOINK
SPARKLE
YES, MA'AM.
ARE YOU READY TO ORDER?
ROGER. ♡
THIS IS AGEHA. THE TSUYU-SAN HAS LANDED.
YOU'VE MET TSUYU'S DAD BEFORE, RIGHT?
WE CAN'T TAKE THE CHANCE THAT YOUR IDENTITY WILL BE REVEALED TO THE GUY SHE'S MEETING.
Right?
NOW THE FUN REALLY STARTS.
Earl grey tea for me.
That'll be right out, Ma'am.
URGH...

ZZT
YUKARI CHECKING IN.
THE ARTISAN HAS ARRIVED AT THE FRONT DESK.
Mic
ROGER THAT. ♪
I'M READY FOR ACTION OVER HERE, TOO.
...
BY THE WAY...
(whisper)
...DID I REALLY HAVE TO DRESS UP AS A WAITER?!
EXCUSE ME.
In the cafe.

TSUYU?
...
IS SOMETHING WRONG?
DAD...
NO.
...I...
WELCOME, ICHIHASHI-SAMA.
Your guest has already arrived.
Lovely!
...

YEP.
Nope, nope.
Nope, nope, nope.
Not a single thing.
That was a fast reply!
OH!
WELL, I GUESS THERE IS SOMETHING.
WHA...
WHAT IS IT?!
I WANT YOU TO COME WITH ME...
...OF YOUR OWN FREE WILL.

OH, THEY'LL ABSOLUTELY LOVE TSUYU-CHAN! ♡
AND TO MARRY INTO A GOOD FAMILY WITHOUT THE BURDEN OF BEING THE WIFE OF THE FAMILY HEAD...! ☆
A true matchmaker.
SHE'S GOING TO TRY TO SEAL THE DEAL...
LET'S BE OFF, SHALL WE?
HEY, SIS...
"HEY, MITSUYA-KUN. ARE YOU SURE THAT THERE'S NOTHING FOR ME TO DO?"

OH, TSUYU...
YOU LOOK BEAUTIFUL.
DAD...
OH, STOP BEING SO MUSHY-GUSHY!!
カクッ
Ouch...
Hi-yah!
IT'S NOT LIKE SHE'S WALKING DOWN THE AISLE THIS INSTANT!
KEEP IT TOGETHER!
Yes, ma'am!
WAIT...
DOES THAT MEAN WE CAN...
...DECLINE THIS OFFER...?

THE DAY OF THE ARRANGED MARRIAGE MEETING
市橋
*Sign=Ichihashi
OH MY!
TSUYU-CHAN, YOU LOOK ABSOLUTELY BEAUTIFUL!! YOUR AUNTIE IS SO PROUD!
How lovely!
YOU WEAR THAT KIMONO WITH SUCH GRACE! I DID A SPECTACULAR JOB DRESSING YOU, IF I DO SAY SO MYSELF!
Come see!
KASUMI-SAN! KASUMI-SAN...!!
TSUYU-CHAN IS READY!
Tsuyu's dad
SST
SIS... YOU DON'T HAVE TO SHOUT, I CAN HEAR Y--

Episode 70

I JUST HOPE THIS WON'T AFFECT OUR REPUTATION.
If you say so.
THEN WE JUST HAVE TO MAKE SURE WE DON'T GET CAUGHT IN THE ACT. ♡
As long as Sekiguchi-san's got our backs. ♪
NO WAY, NO HOW WILL I EVER LET A LOVELESS MARRIAGE TAKE PLACE!
Rawr!
ALL RIGHT...
LET'S GET...
...THIS PARTY STARTED.

HEY, GUYS...
SHOULDN'T WE LET TSUYU-SAN IN ON THIS, TOO?
NAH, IT'S COOL. ♪
Mwa ha ha.
I DON'T WANT TO GIVE HER ANYTHING EXTRA TO WORRY ABOUT.
SURPRISES ARE THE BEST! ♡
You only live once!
HE'S JUST BEING A HUGE GOOFBALL.
...
HEY, C'MON.
ISN'T IT FUN TO BE THE BAD GUYS FOR ONCE? ♪

I REALLY AM A NICE GUY!
YOUR PERSONALITY IS DEFECTIVE.
Ha ha.
AND SO LIKE I TOLD YOU BEFORE I HANDED OUT THE DATA SHEETS, THOSE WILL BE YOUR DUTIES.
Tuned them out.
...
YUKARI-KUN, YOU DON'T LOOK SATISFIED.
Hrmm...
WELL...
...I JUST DON'T QUITE UNDERSTAND...
...WHAT EXACTLY MY ROLE IS.
IF YOU DON'T LIKE IT, AGEHA-CHAN CAN DO IT.
NO WAY!! ANYTHING BUT THAT!

...LET'S DO WHAT WE CAN FOR THEM.
OKEY-DOKEY!
SEVERAL DAYS LATER: STRATEGY MEETING
V·B·R
Here.
HERE'S A PHOTO OF THE GUY, AS WELL AS HIS STATS.
MY RESEARCH TURNED UP A LOT OF INTERESTING TIDBITS.
バサッ
Ohhh.
HE'S THE SECOND SON OF THE CEO OF A MID-SIZED BUSINESS.
WOW!
Oh.
YOU COULD SAY THE SAME ABOUT MITSU.
HE LOOKS LIKE A PRETTY NICE GUY.
GOOD POINT.
HEY, THAT'S NOT VERY NICE!

...GETTING TREATED LIKE SHE'S SOMETHING SPECIAL IS THE KIND OF THING...
...ANY GIRL...
...WOULD LOVE.
もギゅー
HUG
GOSH, SHE'S SO CUTE.
Hwah?!
SQUEEZE
SQUEEZE
ALL RIGHT THEN...

WELL...
...I DON'T KNOW WHAT WE'LL END UP DOING BUT...
...IT'S FOR TSUYU-SAN...
...SO LET'S GO ALL OUT!!
LOOK AT YOU, SO INTO THIS.
PAT
PAT
WHY SHOULDN'T I BE?! KUROMINE-SAN'S ACTUALLY TREATING TSUYU-SAN REALLY NICE!
Kyaa
YOU KNOW...

BRRR
WOOOOOO
ゴゴゴゴゴ
EVER SINCE THAT DAY, HE'S DESPISED SEKIGUCHI.
Yikes!!
SHIVER
SHIVER
IT'S JUST LIKE HOW HE'S REALLY PROTECTIVE OF HIS FOOD.
TSUYU-SAN IS ON THE SAME LEVEL AS FOOD?!
It's not like I can't sympathize with his brand of pettiness.

BY THE WAY, WHY DOES KUROMINE-SAN...
...HATE SEKIGUCHI-SAN SO MUCH?
OHH... THAT...
Mumble Mumble
HUH? IS IT SOMETHING SERIOUS?
Please, who are we talking about?
NO.
THE FIRST TIME THAT SEKIGUCHI AND THE ARTISAN MET...
MY MY, WHAT A BEAUTIFUL LITTLE JAPANESE DOLL WE HAVE HERE. ♡
I'M SEKIGUCHI FROM VILLA ANGE.
Sekiguchi (Age 23)
SO VERY PLEASED TO MAKE YOUR ACQUAINTANCE. ♡
KISS ♡
ERGH!

Sexual harassment.

WOW, WHAT A SURPRISE.
YEAH.
BUT HOW AWESOME IS IT THAT THE TWO OF THEM ARE FINALLY TOGETHER? ♥
Good job, Tsuyu-san! ☆
Well, you know...
I GUESS IT WAS THE RIGHT DECISION TO HAVE HER GO CHECK UP ON MITSU WHILE HE WAS SICK.
DON'T YOU FEEL A BIT BAD THAT SHE ENDED UP GETTING SICK, TOO?
They were just in the same room for a little while and she caught his cold... Kuromine-san's cooties must be extra strong!!
She's innocent.
I WISH I DIDN'T KNOW EXACTLY WHAT THEY WERE DOING.
The Artisan could only strike...
...while Mitsu was still weak from his cold.

WELL, SINCE I'M GOING TO BE BUSY TODAY TRYING TO CATCH UP FOR LOST TIME WHILE I WAS AWAY...
WHY DON'T YOU GO HAVE SOME TEA WITH AGEHA-CHAN?
Really?
TAP
NOPE...
NOT GONNA QUESTION IT.
Let's go, shall we?

SO WE COULD SPEND TIME TOGETHER.
BLUNT
WHY DIDN'T ANYONE TELL ME KUROMINE-SAN WAS REALLY LIKE THIS?!
CALM DOWN, AGEHA!
HE'S JUST BEING COMPLETELY OPEN WITH HIS FEELINGS.
DON'T QUESTION IT!!
Eeeek!!
And with a straight face!!
Isn't there anything that I can help out with?
Hmm?

ニコー
SMILE
YOU DON'T HAVE TO DO A SINGLE THING, TSUYU.
So don't worry even the tiniest bit.
PAT
PAT
...
Um...
Um...
IT'S SO WEIRD TO SEE KUROMINE-SAN BEING NICE TO TSUYU-SAN...
THEN WHAT DID YOU BRING TSUYU-SAN HERE FOR?
HMM?

I'LL DO WHATEVER I HAVE TO. ♡
Tee hee. ♥
THIS GUY IS SCARY WHEN IT COMES TO TSUYU.
Okay...
ME!
ME!
UPER
AGER
WHAT SHALL I DO, SIR?!
THAT SHALL BE DECIDED WITHIN THE NEXT COUPLE OF DAYS. STAND BY AND WAIT FOR YOUR ORDERS!!
ビ
AYE AYE, SIR!!
Idiot brigade
UH...
...UM!
WHAT SHOULD I DO...?

IT'S NO TROUBLE AT ALL!!
WHATEVER IT TAKES TO MAKE YOU HAPPY!
EVEN IF THAT MEANS YOU GETTING MARRIED TO THAT EVIL PERVERT KUROMINE-SAN! I'D SWALLOW MY TEARS AND THROW RICE AT YOUR WEDDING WITH THE BEST OF 'EM!
I'LL DO THIS FOR YOU!!
YAAARRRRRRRRRRRRRRRRRRRRRRR
He gave in.
The sound of enthu-siasm
SO...
...WHAT DO YOU WANT US TO DO?
HMM, YOUR JOB WILL BE...
...GETTING IN TOUCH WITH SEKIGUCHI-SAN AS SOON AS POSSIBLE.
YOU'RE ACTUALLY ASKING SEKIGUCHI ...FOR A FAVOR?
THIS MUST MEAN A LOT TO YOU.
DON'T BE SILLY. ♪
Ha ha.
ちょい
YOU'RE THE ONE ASKING HIM FOR A FAVOR, YUKARI-KUN.

AND YUKARI-KUN, YOU WOULDN'T WANT TO LOSE...
...YOUR PRECIOUS BEAD ARTIST, WOULD YOU?
?!
Argh...
HE'S EVIL TO THE CORE.
Ack!
UM...
UH...
I'M SORRY...
...TO CAUSE YOU ALL THIS TROUBLE.
TSUYU-SAN!!
くわ
RAWR

Taian=an auspicious day in the Japanese calendar

YUKARI-KUN AND AGEHA-CHAN...
...THANKS IN ADVANCE FOR YOUR COOPERATION. ♡
He's so creepy!!!

Hello, this is Banri Hidaka. I just realized that it's already June! Time flies, doesn't it?

I turned 32 on May 31st! I'm enjoying my thirties.
My brain is always filled with work.

Thanks a bunch to all the people who sent birthday cards and presents.

A good friend of mine gave me an adorable cosmetics and hair accessories kit that's in the shape of a matryoshka. Thank you so much! Let's chat soon.

There's a lot of make-up stuffed inside of the matryoshka dolls!

BADUM BADUM
POP

Also, another good friend of mine pulled a hilarious practical joke on me! I'll write about that another time though, when I have the chance. Thanks for the super surprise!
I hope you enjoy my 38th manga volume, V.B. Rose Volume 12!

OH!!
THEN THE ARRANGED MARRIAGE MEETING'S BEEN CALLED OFF?
NOPE.
And that's good, right?
Blunt
PLANS FOR THAT HAVEN'T CHANGED.
SAY WHAT?!!
EXCEPT FOR THE PART...
...WHERE I SABOTAGE IT. ♪
SAY WHAAAT?!!
Sabotage...?

Frm Kana-chan
Sub No title
Die, Kuromine.
KANA-CHAN GAVE ME HER BLESSING. ♡
Aww. ☆
THAT'S A BIG FAT LIE!!!
Aww, Kana-chan... ♡
That cell phone's radiating bad vibes!
...

AHHHH!!
THE OASIS OF MY HEART HAS BEEN CONTAMINATED!
WAAAAAAAAAAH
AH...
AH...
AH...
AGEHA-CHAN?!
Rooting for them, but conflicted.
But congratulations...
Th...Th... Thank you.
HA HA, SORRY WE DIDN'T LET YOU GUYS KNOW SOONER. ♡
NAH.
IT'S YOUR BUSINESS.
Ageha...
Agh!!
DOES KANA-SAN KNOW ABOUT THIS?!
Y...YES.
I JUST CALLED HER TO TELL HER.
KANA-SAAAN!!
DEEDLE-DOOP ♪
WHO'S CELL PHONE IS THAT?
NOT MINE.
OH!
IT'S ME, IT'S ME!
I got it, I got it.

...
AH...
UM...
I'M SORRY...
...THAT I DIDN'T... CONTACT YOU.
UM...
I CAUGHT...
...A COLD.
BLUSH
WHATEVER HAPPENED, HE'S TO BLAME!!
...
Isn't it nice to see girls being friends with each other?

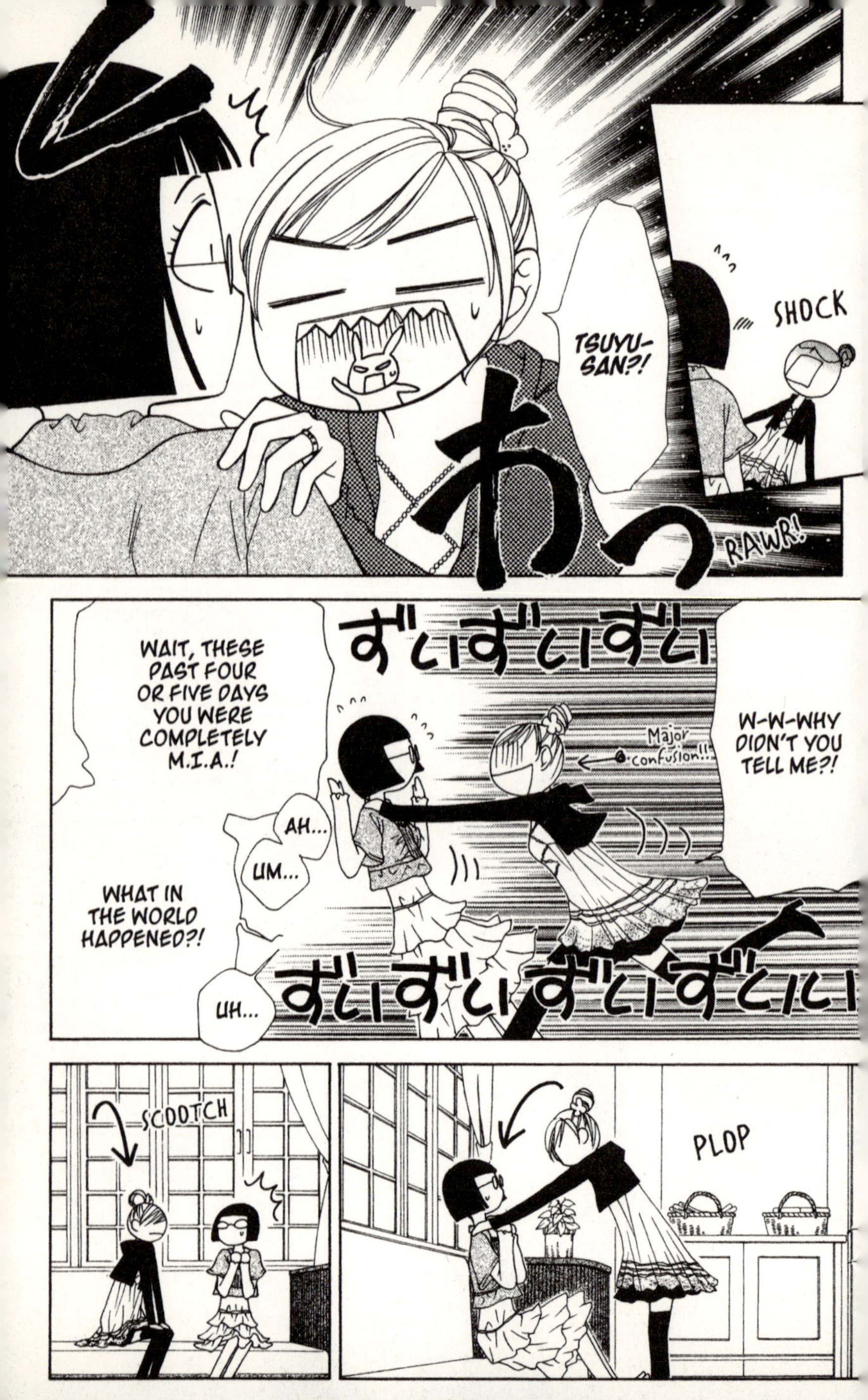

SHOCK
TSUYU-SAN?!
あっ
RAWR!
W-W-WHY DIDN'T YOU TELL ME?!
ずいずいずい
Major confusion!!
WAIT, THESE PAST FOUR OR FIVE DAYS YOU WERE COMPLETELY M.I.A.!
AH...
UM...
WHAT IN THE WORLD HAPPENED?!
UH...
ずいずいずいずいい
PLOP
SCOOTCH

AND SO...
HUG
...NOW THE CAT'S OUT OF THE BAG. ♥
HOCK

B-but... Tsuyu-san...
...y-you were supposed to be coming today, right?
OH.
Y...
YEAH.
もじ...
UM...
MITSUYA-KUN...
...CAME BY MY HOUSE...
...AND PICKED... ME UP...
MITSUYA-KUN?!

"TSUYU?!"
キ...
キィ
H...
HI, GUYS...
WHY WERE YOU HIDING OUT THERE ANYWAY?
B...BECAUSE I WAS EMBARRASSED...
What's with all the flowers in the air?!
EMBARRASSED ABOUT WHAT?!

HEY.
STOP HIDING AND COME OUT HERE...
?
...TSÜYU.

I TAKE THAT BACK, IT'S CRAZIER WHEN YOU'RE HERE.
SCRUB
SCRUB
No one can let their guard down for a second!
WUT?
HEY.
HEY.
ちょんっ
WHAT DOES THIS TEXT MEAN?
THE ONE YOU SENT ME WHILE YOU WERE OUT SICK.
HMM?
From: Kuromine-san
Subject: I'm going to do something about the arranged marriage meeting.
This
YOU'RE...
...TALKING ABOUT TSUYU-SAN'S MEETING, RIGHT?
WHAT HAVE YOU GOT IN MIND?!
Ohh.
HOLD UP, HOLD UP.
LET ME START FROM THE BEGINNING. ♪

Why is he ☆ so happy?
YAY, KUROMINE-SAN! YOU'RE BACK!!
WERE YOU LONELY WITHOUT ME?
IT WAS CRAZY BUSY WITHOUT YOU, MAN.
AGEHA-CHAN, YOU DOLL! ♡
A kiss on the cheek.
AND YUKARI-KUN, YOU BEAUTIFUL ANGEL! ♡
A kiss on the lips (almost).

AFTER ONE WEEK OF SICK LEAVE...
... KUROMINE-SAN TRIUMPHANTLY RETURNED TO VBR!!
SPARKLE
SPARKLE
HELLO, EVERY-BODY!
MII-KUN IS BACK IN BUSINESS! ♡

Episode 69

HUH?!
GRIN ♥
ニッ
I'LL SABOTAGE...
...THAT ARRANGED MARRIAGE MEETING.

TSUYU ...
ちゅ
SMOOC
っ
MM.
ちゅう~~~っ
SMACK
MM.
MMM.
Ohh...
Ooh...
BADUM
BADUM
...MI...
DON'T WORRY.
Your kisses are so p-passionate.

I NEVER...
...EVER WANT TO LEAVE YOU AGAIN.

BUT I LOVE YOU.
I REALLY LOVE YOU, MITSUYA-KUN.

EVER SINCE THAT DAY IN SIXTH GRADE...
I'M SORRY.
...I'VE BEEN WANTING TO DRAIN AWAY...
...ALL MY UNEXPRESSED FEELINGS FOR YOU.
I KNEW I HAD TO...
...all things...
...come to an end...
...TAKE CONTROL OF MY EMOTIONS.

I...
...I'VE ALWAYS LET OTHER PEOPLE BE IN CHARGE OF MY LIFE.
BUT I...
...DON'T LIKE...
...THAT ABOUT MYSELF.
I TOLD MYSELF THAT I HAD TO...
...FORGET ABOUT YOU.

MITSUYA-KUN!
MITSUYA-KUN...!
I DON'T KNOW WHAT TO DO.
I DON'T KNOW HOW TO DECLINE...
...AN ARRANGED MARRIAGE MEETING...
I...!

NN ....
MI ...
MI... TSU...
MITSUYA... KUN.

KURO--
SAY MY NAME LIKE YOU USED TO...
...TSUYU.

KUROMINE-KU...
...NN.

DON'T RUN AWAY.
DON'T EVER...
...LEAVE ME AGAIN.
HUG

I'M NOT A KID ANYMORE.
I CAN'T BLINDLY OBEY WHAT PEOPLE TELL ME.
I'M SORRY.
I DON'T WANT TO BE A GOOD BOY.

KUROMINE ...KUN...
I...I...

KURO--
MM
...

DON'T LEAVE ME.
I'VE ALWAYS LOVED YOU.

DON'T GET MARRIED.
...
WHY WOULD YOU DO THAT TO ME?
DO YOU WANT TO SEE ME RUN AROUND IN CIRCLES AGAIN?

COUGH
HACK
KAFF
KUROMINE-KUN?!
KUROMINE-KUN, ARE YOU ALL RIGHT?!!
WE'VE GOT TO GET YOU BACK TO BED...
COUGH!
BADUM

I...I NEED TO GO HOME NOW!
NOW WAIT JUST A--
THUD...

NOW THAT YOU CAN USE "SEEING AGEHA-CHAN" AS YOUR COVER...
...YOU'VE STARTED COMING OVER TO VBR A LOT MORE OFTEN!
JUST TRY TO DENY IT!

BESIDES, YOU THINK I DON'T KNOW WHAT YOU'RE FEELING?! THINK AGAIN!
BLUSH
I'M NOT LIKE YUKARI-KUN AND THE REST--I CAN READ PEOPLE.
YOU BEST OF ALL.
I KNOW WHAT YOU'RE UP TO.

L-LIVING IN A RURAL AREA...
...YOU GET A LOT OF OFFERS FOR ARRANGED MARRIAGE MEETINGS.
THAT'S NOT WHAT I'M ASKING!!
Ha...ha...
TWITCH
WHY ARE YOU ALWAYS LIKE THAT?
YOU ALWAYS TRAMPLE OVER MY FEELINGS!
KURO--
YOU KNOW WHERE I'M COMING FROM, DON'T YOU?!
オロ
オロ

I HEARD THAT YOU'RE GOING TO HAVE AN ARRANGED MARRIAGE MEETING.
WHY ARE YOU DOING THAT?

YUKARI-KUN!!
IT REALLY WARMED MY HEART...
...TO HEAR THAT.
I had to say thank you...
I THOUGHT THAT YOU DIDN'T LIKE ME.
How dare he spill my secrets!!
HUH?!
I WOULD NEVER WASTE TIME TALKING TO PEOPLE I DON'T LIKE!
REALLY?
B...
But...
But...
No buts!
Example
Sekiguchi
Hmm, Kuromine doesn't like me.
Oh.
Ha...
I'M GLAD...
...TO FINALLY HEAR YOU SAY THAT.

UMM...
...ARISAKA-KUN TOLD ME SOMETHING I DIDN'T KNOW...
...ABOUT THE TIME I BROKE MY ANKLE.
THANK YOU FOR THE FLOWER BASKET.
I NEVER WOULD HAVE GUESS THAT YOU SENT IT...
Um...
ぶほっ
GLARGH!
A nice push...
...in the right direction!
K... KUROMINE-KUN, ARE YOU ALL RIGHT?!
KAFF
HAKKK
COUGH
COUGH!
Oh...
I can see his face so clearly.

P...
PLOP
K... KUROMINE-KUN...
HOW...
...ARE YOU FEELING?
JUST ...
...THE WAY IT LOOKS.

Tsuyu's boundary line.
...
おず…
FIND A PLACE TO SIT.
ビクッ
TWITCH
...

THEN YOUR MOTHER CAME OUT ON HER WAY SHOPPING.
BADUM
Oh my goodness!
Is that you, Tsuyu-chan?!
SHE RECOGNIZED ME...
Squee! Look at you! You're so pretty and grown-up!
Don't just stand out there! Come in, come in!
...AND LET ME INTO THE HOUSE.
ぐいぐい
UH... UM...
AND??
HUGGLE
OH NO!
SHOULD I HAVE NOT COME IN THE FIRST PLACE?
DON'T STAND THERE.
YOU SHOULD ...
...COME IN.
WHAT?!

WHY ARE YOU...
ARF!
のしっ
RUFF
RUFF
TSUYAKO ...
SO YOU REMEMBER ME, TOO.
"TOO"?
I...
...I WAS...
...STAND-ING OUTSIDE THE DOOR...
...BECAUSE I WAS TOO SCARED TO RING THE DOORBELL.

ICHIHASHI ...?

Episode 68

WERE YOU WORRIED ABOUT ME?
もきゅー
HUG
Good girl!
DON'T WORRY, I'M GONNA BE FINE.
ARF. ♡
...
ICHIHASHI?

ごろ…
WHY DO THINGS...
...NEVER WORK OUT THE WAY I WANT THEM TO?
KNOCK
KNOCK
もそ…
…
WHO IS IT?
キイ
ARF!
TSUYAKO!
Phew.

I'VE ALWAYS LOVED SPENDING TIME WITH YOU.
ANOTHER DREAM...
"IT'S YOUR FAULT FOR HIDING YOUR FEELINGS..."
"...AND HARASSING HER LIKE A LITTLE BOY!!"
"TSUYU-SAN IS GOING TO HAVE AN ARRANGED MARRIAGE MEETING!"

I MANIPULATED THAT GUILT TO TIE DOWN YOUR HEART.
So you cut your hair.
It looks like a helmet.
What?! A helmet?!
Ha ha. A nice helmet.
I RELISHED HAVING A HOLD ON YOU AGAIN.
IT DIDN'T MATTER TO ME THAT I HAD TO PLAY THE BAD GUY.
ACK!
BECAUSE I'VE ALWAYS LOVED IT...
Leaving so soon?
You just got here.
CLENCH

...TO TREAT YOU BACK.
ICHIHASHI.
YOU HAVEN'T CHANGED AT ALL.
I KNEW HOW TO ENSNARE YOU...
..SO THAT YOU WOULDN'T BE ABLE TO RUN AWAY AGAIN.
I SAW IT.
I SAW YOUR OVERWHELMING...
.GUILT.

BUT YOU ...
ARTISAN?
...YOU RAN AWAY AGAIN.
What are you doing back there?
PEEK
PEEK
YOU RAN AWAY FROM ME.
BUT I WASN'T THE SAME OLD ME.
NOW, I KNEW HOW...

WHAT?
YOU KNOW EACH OTHER?
DO YOU KNOW...
WHAT'S WRONG, ARTISAN?
...HOW I FELT ...
...AT THAT MOMENT WE REUNITED?

I LIKED HEARING ABOUT THE ARTISAN...
じゃーーーん
BEHOLD! HER NEWEST CREATION! ♡
NICE! ♡ I WANNA SEE! ♪
What, what?
THE ARTISAN HAS AN ADMIRATION FOR THE FEMALE FORM...
...SO THE OTHER DAY WE GOT ALL WOUND UP TALKING ABOUT HOW SHORT SKIRTS SHOULD BE FOR GIRLS' SCHOOL UNIFORMS.
Heh heh.
Huh?
BUT WE NEVER TALK ABOUT THAT KIND OF STUFF...
...BUT NEVER IN A MILLION YEARS...
...COULD I HAVE IMAGINED THAT THIS MYTHICAL CREATURE...
She says she likes this guy's books.
Lifestyl
Fashion
Really? We'd probably get along. ♡
I think so.
...WAS SOMEONE I ALREADY KNEW.
SECOND YEAR OF HIGH SCHOOL, SPRING

SO, WHAT'S HER NAME?
"THE ARTISAN"?
CONFIDENCE
IN OTHER WORDS, YOU HAVE NO IDEA.
Forget I asked.
IS SHE CUTE?
I HAVE A PRETTY LIBERAL IDEA OF "CUTE."
THENNN... I'LL JUST LET THAT BE A SURPRISE WHEN I MEET HER.
YUKARI-KUN STARTED TELLING ME STORIES ABOUT "THE ARTISAN"...

WHAT?! NO WAY, A CROWN?!
IT'S GOOD ENOUGH TO SELL!
I KNOW, RIGHT?!
SHE LIVES A LITTLE FAR AWAY ...
NICE! I CAN'T WAIT TO MEET HER!
...BUT I'LL BRING HER TO THE STORE SOMETIME.

HE JUST GETS MORE BEAUTIFUL ALL THE TIME...
Glowing with youthful beauty
SO...
...WHO'S THIS COOL PERSON YOU MET?
OH YEAH! WELL, SHE'S THIS GIRL IN MY GRADE.
SHE WEARS GLASSES AND SHE'S SUPER CLUMSY...
...BUT IF YOU GIVE HER SOME BEADS, SHE'S LIKE A MACHINE!!
You're not really selling her...
HOW DO YOU KNOW ABOUT THE BEADS?
I ASKED HER TO MAKE A TIARA OR SOMETHING, JUST TO SEE WHAT SHE COULD DO...
...AND BAM! SHE MADE THIS RIGHT IN FRONT OF ME! ♪
Oh good, I didn't smoosh it. ♪
KA-TINK

WHAT?
Is there something on my face?
UM...
NO...
ACTUALLY, DID YOU GET TALLE AGAIN, YUKARI-KUN
♪
YOU NOTICED?
Yukari Arisaka High school Freshman
Fall 168cm tal
I'M GOING TO BE AS TALL AS MY DAD SOON. ♪
Daddy Aoi is 173cm

YUKARI-KUN ...
...PULLED ME OUT OF MY DEPRESSION.
AND THEN CAME HIGH SCHOOL ...
MITSU!!
I MET SOMEBODY REALLY COOL TODAY!

MY SCARRED HEART HURT TOO MUCH TO FEEL ANYBODY ELSE'S PAIN.
HOW ANNOYING ...
THE ONLY ONE WHO COULD CUT ME SO DEEP...
...WAS ICHIHASHI.
IT WAS AROUND THAT TIME...
COOL.
...THAT I HAD A LIFE-CHANGING EXPERIENCE.

I...
...DON'T KNOW WHO YOU ARE.
BLUSH

I DID SOME PRETTY HORRIBLE THINGS TO GIRLS WHO HAD NOTHING TO DO WITH IT.
KUROMINE-KUN, I'VE ALWAYS LIKED YOU!
W...WILL YOU PLEASE GO OUT WITH ME?

ACTUALLY ...
...I WAS IN DESPAIR BECAUSE I DID CARE.
I WAS STILL ATTACHED TO ICHIHASHI.

WAVE WAVE
SQUEE!! HE'S SUCH A CUTIE-PIE!
DANG! YOU'RE SO POPULAR, KUROMINE.
ARE THOSE GIRLS SEVENTH GRADERS?
Cutie-pie is NOT a compliment for a guy.
I GUESS EVERYONE THINKS HE'S COOL.
RUMOR HAD IT...
...ICHIHASHI'S PARENTS GOT A DIVORCE BECAUSE OF HER MOM...
...AND SHE AND HER DAD MOVED AWAY.
ME, I WAS WALLOWING IN DESPAIR.
A movie? Sure, let's go.
Really?!
I JUST DIDN'T...
...CARE ABOUT ANYTHING ANYMORE.
Yay!

...AND THE SUN DIDN'T BREAK THROUGH...
...UNTIL I WAS IN MIDDLE SCHOOL.
KUROMINE-KUN!
Oh.

SHAKE
NO...
...SHE'S NOT LIKE THAT.
WHY...
...DIDN'T YOU TELL ME ANYTHING?
A DARK CLOUD SETTLED OVER MY HEART...

"I'M SORRY."
BADUM
ずる
ずる
OH MY GOSH, WHAT A RELIEF!
IS THIS HOW SHE FELT WHEN SHE REJECTED ME?!

OH MY GOSH, WHAT A RELIEF!
ずる
ずるる
GIMME A BREAK.

BLUSH
What's wrong?
N... Nothing.
I WISH THIS WAS OVER...
ONE WEEK LATER
SORRY.
I'M SORRY, BUT ...
... I JUST CAN'T.

Arooo
OH MAN...
WHY'D THAT GIRL HAVE TO ASK NOW OF ALL TIMES?
Ughh...
"I'M SORRY."
WHY ...
...DID YOU LEAVE WITHOUT SAYING ANYTHING?
6 - 1
Good morning!
Morning.

THEN...
...GIVE ME A WEEK.
KUROMINE
くきゅ〜〜〜〜〜ぇ〜
Whiiiiiiine

...I THINK I WAS IN MORE PAIN BACK THEN.
I LIKE YOU, KUROMINE-KUN.
UM...
YOU DON'T HAVE TO GIVE ME AN ANSWER RIGHT AWAY!

COUGH...
...
HACK
KAFF
HYUK
COUGH
OH GOD, IT HURTS!!!
HAVING A COLD REALLY SUCKS...
ぐったり
KOFF
SSWF...
BUT ICHIHASHI...

...
A NIGHTMARE...
もぞ

ICHIHASHI WAS GONE.
I DIDN'T WANT TO FACE IT...
...BUT I COULDN'T ESCAPE THE TRUTH.

Episode 67

THAT MOMENT...
...SOMETHING BROKE DEEP INSIDE ME.

BUT THE NEXT DAY...
IT'S SAD TO SAY THIS SO CLOSE TO GRADUATION...
...BUT ICHIHASHI-SAN HAS TRANSFERRED TO ANOTHER SCHOOL.
ざわ
WHY DIDN'T SHE TELL ME?!
I COULDN'T PROCESS IT.
MY MIND DREW A BLANK.

I WAS SO CONFUSED.

I'M SORRY.

WHAT'S THE MATTER?
Mumble
YOU'LL SEE TOMORROW.
WHAT?
ABOUT WHAT YOU ASKED ME...
BADUM

I REALLY WAS
CLUELESS.
AFTER A WEEK HAD PASSED...
YOU'VE BEEN DISTANT LATELY.
DID SOMETHING HAPPEN?
...YEAH.
I WAS REALLY BUSY...
...WITH THINGS AT HOME.

I GUESS I SHOULDN'T HAVE KISSED HER OUT OF THE BLUE LIKE THAT.
But I couldn't help it.
Arf!
Arf!
WHAT'S WITH THE "WEEK"?
BLUSH
Kiss on replay.
?
PWUMPF
HOW SHOULD I ACT AROUND HER TOMORROW?

CAN YOU TELL ME...
THAT FLICKER OF A SMILE GAVE ME SUCH HIGH HOPES...
!...
...HOW YOU FEEL?
CAN YOU GIVE ME A WEEK?
...WHICH WERE THEN DASHED.

I THINK YOU ALREADY KNOW, BUT...
...I REALLY LIKE YOU.

I STILL HAVEN'T FIGURED OUT WHY...
...ICHIHASHI CRIED THAT DAY.
LIKE I SAID, I DIDN'T HAVE THE SLIGHTEST IDEA OF WHAT SHE WAS GOING THROUGH.

THEN ONE DAY, CLOSE TO GRADUATION...
KUROMINE
YOU'VE BEEN LOOKING KINDA SAD LATELY.
IS SOMETHING GOING ON?

NOW THAT I KNOW...
...WHAT WAS GOING ON AT THE TIME...
I'm sorry I took number one.
Straight-A student
5
Ha ha ha. I could never be number one.
C-student
3
...I REALIZE THAT HER MOTHER'S SELFISHNESS WAS AT ITS PEAK RIGHT THEN.
AT THE TIME, I WAS CLUELESS.
SO CLUELESS.
Come over next time, then.
I will!
SO VERY CLUELESS.
AND THEN CAME THAT DAY...

THAT'S NOT TRUE.
YOU'RE LIKE...IN THE MIDDLE OF THE MIDDLE.
SINCERE
HA HA HA HA HA HA!
Yeah! I am!
SIGH...
BUT MY MOM...
...DOESN'T CARE UNLESS I'M "NUMBER ONE."

WHOA?!
びくっ
SHE'S BEEN SO SPACEY THESE DAYS.
ARE YOU COMING BY MY PLACE?
OH, UM...
...I...I'M SORRY.
I'VE BEEN TOLD...I HAVE TO COME HOME EARLY FOR A WHILE...
MY MOM...
...TOLD ME I NEED TO STOP PLAYING SO MUCH...
...AND START STUDYING HARDER.
GRIT
I'M NOT THAT SMART, SO...
Heh heh.
!

IT FELT EASY. IT FELT GOOD.
HOW WAS I TO KNOW THAT WHEN WE HIT SIXTH GRADE...
...THINGS WOULD...
...FALL APART.
6 - 1
COMING OVER AGAIN TODAY?
TAP TAP

Do you... think I'm weird?!
Nope!
Heh heh.
SOON WE WERE TOGETHER ALL THE TIME.

STARE
SWIP
Hey!
...
PEEK

I KNEW HOW POSSESSIVE I WAS BEING ABOUT HER.
You really do have a lot of books!
Read anything you want.
You'll never be bored when you're here.
I WANTED HER TO BE FRIENDS WITH ME AND NO ONE ELSE.
SOON IT WASN'T JUST AFTER SCHOOL...
Shizuya-kun, say "Ahh."
Lucky.
Ahh!
...BUT ALSO ON THE WEEKENDS.
I WAS ALWAYS ASKING HER TO HANG OUT WITH ME.
Take a look at this.
Wow!
ICHIHASHI DIDN'T REALLY LIKE TALKING ABOUT HER FAMILY...
...BUT THAT DIDN'T MATTER TO ME.

LUCKY FOR ME...
...ICHIHASHI ALWAYS STAYED LATE. SHE SAID SHE WAS KILLING TIME BEFORE SHE WAS SUPPOSED TO GO HOME.
BING BONG
What!? You're still here?!
Just got out of the student council meeting.
BING BONG
Y... Yeah.
I'm always here.
Eheh...
IT TURNED OUT THAT SHE REALLY DID HAVE TROUBLE MAKING FRIENDS...
...SO I KNEW I HAD MY CHANCE.
Forget staying at school.
Come play at my place.
A...Are you sure?!
YOINK
Of course I'm sure!
I WANTED TO LEARN WHATEVER I COULD ABOUT HER.

ISN'T THAT A GREAT SERIES?
I'M READING IT, TOO.
YOU MUST LIKE READING.

?
SWIP
SWIP
HEE
HEE
HEE

IT'S HER!
ばっ
...SHE'S SITTING ALONE IN THE CLASS-ROOM AFTER SCHOOL AGAIN.
I DON'T THINK SHE HAS ANY FRIENDS.
...
ACTUALLY SHE'S LIKE... ALWAYS ALONE?
BADUM BADUM

I WAS ALWAYS...
DON'T FORGET THE STUDENT COUNCIL MEETING, KUROMINÉ-KUN.
I'LL MEET YOU THERE.
I FORGOT SOMETHING IN THE CLASS-ROOM.
OKAY.
4-1
カラ…
...LOOKING AT YOU.

HA HA!
Opposite of a model brother.
THUD THUD
KERPLUNK
Yeeeeek!!
He tries so hard.
Fell down the stairs.
I HATE YOU!
Waaaah!
GRAB
GRAB
FWUMP

HEY...
MODEL BROTHER
... WANT SOME PORRIDGE?
SHIZUYA ...
C'MERE!
C'MERE!
SHI-CHAN!
?!
LEMME GET RID OF MY COLD BY GIVING IT TO YOU!
Show me how much you love me!
KOFF!
COUGH!
HACK!
HACK!
Yeeep!!!
DON'T! MY COLLEGE ENTRANCE EXAMS ARE COMING UP!
SMOOCH
Nooo!

TSUYU-SAN...
Sniff
...YOU'RE JUMPING INTO THINGS TOO FAST.
KUROMINE
KNOCK
...
KNOCK

I WONDER IF THINGS ARE GOING TO TURN OUT WELL FOR KUROMINE-SAN...
I JUST SAID...
Are you still on that?
...AND TSUYU-SAN.
...
THAT'S BETWEEN THE TWO OF THEM.
WE CAN'T LIVE THEIR LIVES FOR THEM.
ERGH...
BIP
BUT IT CAN'T HURT TO GIVE THEM A NICE PUSH IN THE RIGHT DIRECTION.
BIP
BIP
HUH?
RING
RING

I WONDER IF KUROMINE-SAN IS DOING OKAY?
SIZE S
HE JUST CAUGHT THE COLD THAT'S GOING AROUND.
THE DOCTOR SAID HE'LL RECOVER IN A COUPLE OF DAYS.
IMPRISONED
Waaah! Yukari-kun, you're so mean!
HE'S IN GOOD HANDS AT HIS PARENTS' HOUSE.
Arf.
Watch dog
Since he would start working if he were at the store.
Good call.
Hmm...

FOR THE LONGEST TIME...
...I'VE BEEN CAPTIVATED...
...BY YOUR DOWNCAST EXPRESSION..

Episode 66

Contents

V.B. Rose

Episode 66 5
Episode 67 35
Episode 68 65
Episode 69 95
Episode 70 125
Episode 71 155
Banri Hidaka's Everyday Heaven 185

VB Rose™

Volume 12

By Banri Hidaka

TOKYOPOP®

HAMBURG // LONDON // LOS ANGELES // TOKYO

V.B. Rose Volume 12

Created by Banri Hidaka

Translation - Lori Riser
English Adaptation - Hope Donovan
Retouch and Lettering - Star Print Brokers
Graphic Designer - Amy Martin

Editor - Daniella Orihuela-Gruber
Print Production Manager - Lucas Rivera
Managing Editor - Vy Nguyen
Senior Designer - Louis Csontos
Director of Sales and Manufacturing - Allyson De Simone
Senior Vice President - Mike Kiley
President and C.O.O. - John Parker
C.E.O. and Chief Creative Officer - Stu Levy

A TOKYOPOP® Manga

TOKYOPOP and [logo] are trademarks or registered trademarks of TOKYOPOP Inc.

TOKYOPOP Inc.
5900 Wilshire Blvd. Suite 2000
Los Angeles, CA 90036

E-mail: info@TOKYOPOP.com
Come visit us online at www.TOKYOPOP.com

V. B. ROSE by Banri Hidaka © 2008 Banri Hidaka All rights reserved. First published in Japan in 2008 by HAKUSENSHA, INC., Tokyo English language translation rights in the United States of America, Canada and the United Kingdom arranged with HAKUSENSHA, INC., Tokyo through Tuttle-Mori Agency Inc., Tokyo English text copyright © 2011 TOKYOPOP Inc.

All rights reserved. No portion of this book may be reproduced or transmitted in any form or by any means without written permission from the copyright holders. This manga is a work of fiction. Any resemblance to actual events or locales or persons, living or dead, is entirely coincidental.

ISBN: 978-1-4278-1587-3

First TOKYOPOP printing: April 2011

10 9 8 7 6 5 4 3 2 1

Printed in the USA

VB Rose

Volume 12

Banri Hidaka

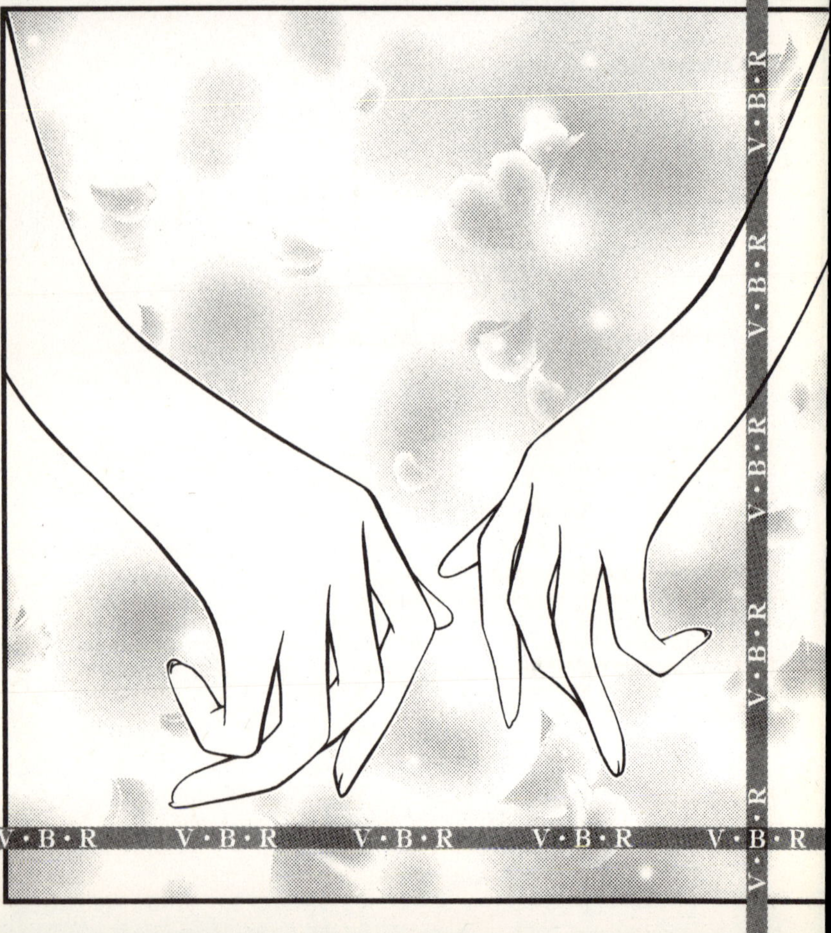